WILBUR
the Wagon's
BIG DREAM

JAMES CONTRERAS

Illustrated by Lynda Farrington Wilson

WILBUR THE WAGON'S BIG DREAM

© 2019 James Contreras

Edited by Karen Contreras

Illustrated by Lynda Farrington Wilson

www.lyndafarringtonwilson.com

ISBN # 978-1-7342569-0-1

DEDICATION

Thank you –

My Mom and Dad

My nephew – for inspiring me
to write a children's book for you.

On a farm in the country where donkeys hee-haw,
Lived the cutest little wagon you ever saw.

Wilbur was his name all red and white,
and shiny all over, a beautiful sight!

His friends were the pigs and the sheep and the cows,
He loved the hay fields...and the tractors and plows.

At sunrise he loved how his world came alive,
With bees buzzing and swarming at all of their hives.

But Wilbur looked east as the sun rose each day,
He dreamed of the beach so far, far away.

He wondered about the fishes and shore,
and seagulls and sand... a new world to explore!

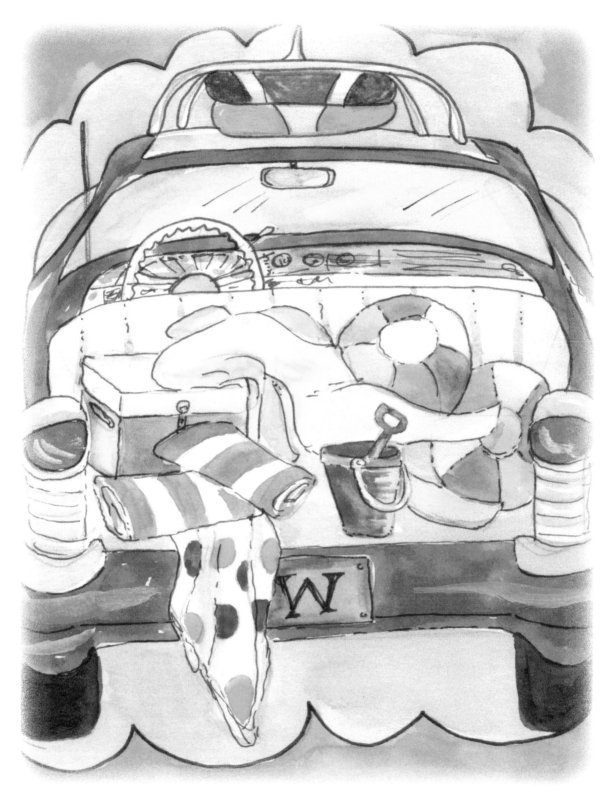

He pictured his roof with surfboards and racks,
and inside his tailgate were wetsuits he packed.

Wilbur just knew he was meant for the beach,
but was his big dream too far out of reach?

The road to the beach was winding and long,
but somehow brave Wilbur just knew he'd belong.

So he talked to his parents when he wanted to go,
his Mom Marla Mercury and his Dad Chrysler Moe.
They told Wilbur the Wagon, "You're ready to go,
explore your new world, but be sure to drive slow!"

So Wilbur got ready, as any car would,
checked his wipers and tires and under the hood.
On the day of his journey his parents said bye,
with their toots and beep-beeps, and lights flashing high.

So Wilbur the wagon was off-heading east,
exploring the country... his longing had ceased.
The road east was bumpy, then narrow, then wide...
at times Wilbur wished for a map at his side.

A few hours later Wilbur stopped for a snack,
he met a new friend, and old truck named Mack.
Mack told Wilbur to follow the clouds,
and through the mountains...He did! It worked! And he was so proud!

He continued along windows down, music playing,
saw great sights and sounds, just like Mack had been saying.

Up high in the mountains, it started to snow...
Wilbur wondered, "What now!?". He has nowhere to go.

He pulled up to a diner with lots of cars there,
"What luck", he exclaimed, "in the heart of nowhere!"

He stopped for some gas and a warm cup of tea,
told his waitress Betty Beetle where he hoped he would be,
"The beach is the place I am longing to go.....
so far my long journey is moving too slow."

Betty Beetle was wise as wise as can be,
she had some advice for Wilbur's journey.
"Take your time", Betty said, "Enjoy the whole ride,
do not speed way up like a roaring rip tide.
There's plenty of time to enjoy the sea,
but savor the ride... your journey, with glee."

So Wilbur moved on and started to smile,
knowing full well he'd enjoy every mile.
Wilbur stayed focused and continued to drive,
slowed down on his speed and was feeling alive!

When Wilbur was only a few miles to shore…..
He met Dune Buggy Dougie, who helped him some more.

Dougie pointed him toward the sandy sea shore,
and as fast as a wink he saw surfers galore!

Wilbur parked by the guard stand, near surfboards and towels.
The boards all came running to greet him with howls!
"Dear Wilbur, our new friend, where have you been!?
You belong here with us, you'll always fit in!"

Not before long, his roof held surfboards galore,
just like he had dreamed in his farm life, before.
He loved his farm life, but knew in his heart
that the beach was his place to make a clean start.

You might ask what lessons were learned on the way,
'follow your heart' is what he would say.
'There may be obstacles that stand in the way,
but you have to be happy at the end of the day.'

So Wilbur the Wagon enjoyed his new friends...
he thrived at the beach! For now, that's the end!

AUTHOR, JAMES CONTRERAS AND WILBUR

Dan Przygocki, Photographer

Made in the USA
Middletown, DE
26 November 2019